Harry's Stormy Night

Harry's Stormy Night

UNA LEAVY

illustrated by PETER UTTON

MARGARET K. McELDERRY BOOKS

For my husband,
Lorcan,
with love
U.L.

For Harvey, Lesley, and Harriet
P.U.

First United States edition 1995

Margaret K. McElderry Books
An imprint of Simon & Schuster Children's Publishing Division
1230 Avenue of the Americas
New York, New York 10020

First published 1994 by Orchard Books, London

Printed in Belgium

10 9 8 7 6 5 4 3 2 1

The text of this book is set in Garamond.
The illustrations are rendered in watercolor.

Library of Congress Cataloging-in-Publication Data

Leavy, Una.
Harry's stormy night / Una Leavy ; illustrated by Peter Utton. — 1st U.S. ed.
p. cm.
Summary: When a big storm knocks out their electricity, Harry's family sings and tells stories by candlelight.
ISBN 0-689-50625-2
[1. Storms—Fiction. 2. Stories in rhyme.] I. Utton, Peter, ill. II. Title.
PZ8.3.L48Har 1995
[E]—dc20 94-12772

All evening the North wind roared.

Harry had never heard such wind,
whistling around chimneys,
ripping through branches,
whipping at branches
over his head.

His mother tapped at the window.
"Come in, Harry," she said.
"It's getting very wild
and soon it will be night.
Time to be inside."

It was warm inside,
Baby Tom asleep and
only the storm for noise.

Just then Daddy came in.
"There's a tree down," he said.
"It brought some wires with it,
and the wind is rising. There'll
be no power tonight."

But the stove
was warm, and the kettle
was singing gently.
They put candles
in the candlesticks
and settled down
for a long stormy night.

Mom made an apple tart.
Harry helped with the pastry,
rolling it this way and that.

All the time
wind boomed at the windows,
branches tapped at the glass.
Baby Tom awoke,
chewing his fingers
and crying for his food.

Harry held him
while Mom warmed his milk.
His eyes were wide
with the soft mellow light
and the great noise outside.

They washed up after supper
and put the baby to bed.
There was no TV
so Harry made his own
pictures instead.

And Mom told him stories
of times long past when
she was a little girl, while
outside the wind still whirled
and Harry was sleepy at last.

Into bed then
where Teddy lay
under the bedclothes.
The branches rattled the
windowpane, and
the wind howled.
Harry held Teddy close.

In the shadowy moonlight,
everything in the room
looked strange.
Where was the bookshelf
with Harry's storybooks?
His robot collection,
his trucks and transformers
—why did they seem to move?

Harry thumped the pillow,
pulled the quilt to his chin.
“Don’t be scared, Teddy,”
he said. “I’ll just tuck you in.”

What was that?
A little cry came
over the roar of the storm.

“Baby Tom’s awake!
He’ll be scared!”
Harry hopped out of bed.

The baby's room
was full of moonlight.

"Don't cry," Harry said.
"It's all right.
It's just a stormy night."

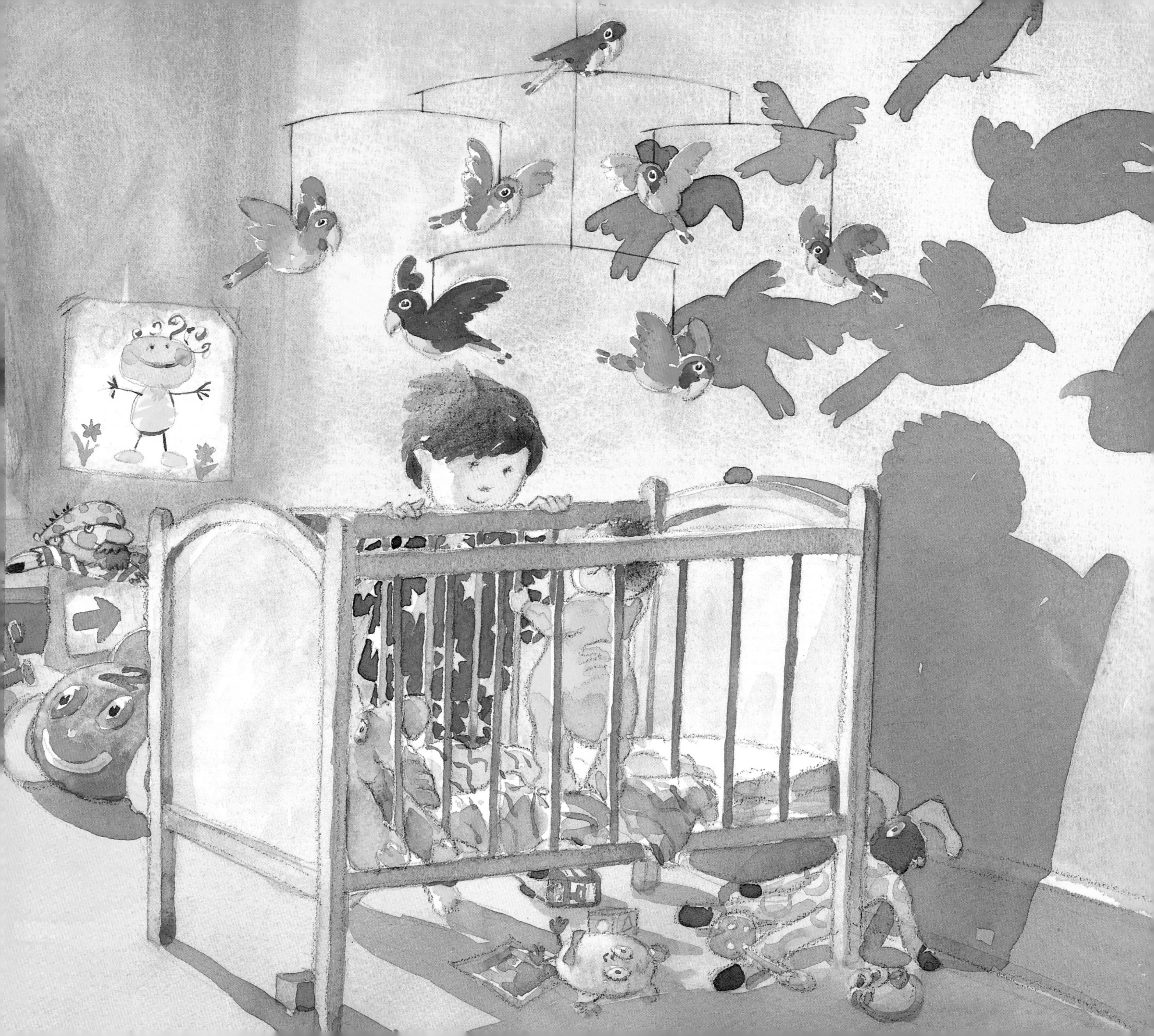

Harry couldn't lift Tom
from his crib
so he sat on the floor
and over the roar of the wind
he began to sing.

Then he told him stories
as shadows drifted past,
while outside
the wind still whirled
and Baby Tom
was sleepy at last.

2

That's what Mom saw
when she hurried upstairs
and opened the door—
baby snug in his crib,
Harry asleep on the floor.

Mom smiled
as she tucked in her boys.
It was warm inside,
the children asleep

and only the storm for noise.